Peppa Pig™

George's First Day at Playgroup

Today is George's first day at playgroup.
"Isn't George too small for playgroup?" asks Peppa.
"You can look after him," says Daddy Pig.
Peppa isn't sure she wants George at
her playgroup, but she likes the idea of
looking after him.

Now it is time to go home. "What will you paint next time, George?" asks Madame Gazelle. "Dine-saw! Grrr!" giggles George. "Hee, hee, hee!" everyone laughs.

"I've painted a flower," says Peppa.

"Very good, Peppa," smiles Madame Gazelle.

"And look, George has painted a dinosaur."

Madame Gazelle sticks Peppa and George's

pictures on the wall.

Peppa admires her flower painting.
"Perfect," she says, happily.
George is still painting. Instead of a stalk
and leaves he has painted another circle
with five lines sticking out from it.
"You are doing it all wrong!" says Peppa.

George draws a big green circle.

"No, George. That's the wrong colour,"
snorts Peppa. "Watch me."

Peppa makes yellow petal shapes.

George paints a green zigzag.

"George! That's the wrong shape," says Peppa.

Peppa carefully dips her brush into a pot of
pink paint and draws a big pink circle
right in the middle of her paper.

"Watch me, George," snorts Peppa.
"First, you paint a big circle."

George shakes his toy, Mr Dinosaur, at Madame Gazelle, "Grrr! Dine-saw!" "Aah! Really scary!" laughs Madame Gazelle. Peppa is proud of George making everyone laugh. "George is my little brother. He's brilliant," she says.

Here is Madame Gazelle, Peppa's playgroup teacher. She looks after Peppa and her friends. Madame Gazelle tells the children that George is coming to play. The children are all very excited about meeting Peppa's little brother.

"Are you sure George is big enough?"
Peppa asks when they arrive.
"Yes, he'll be fine," replies Daddy Pig.
"OK. He can come," says Peppa.
She holds onto George's hand.
"Grunt! Grunt!" snorts George, jumping
up and down.